The Silver Moon

LULLABIES AND CRADLE SONGS

POEMS BY
Jack Prelutsky

ILLUSTRATED BY
Jui Ishida

Greenwillow Books   *An Imprint of HarperCollinsPublishers*

The Silver Moon: Lullabies and Cradle Songs
Text and music copyright © 2013 by Jack Prelutsky
Illustrations copyright © 2013 by Jui Ishida
All rights reserved. Manufactured in China.
For information address HarperCollins Children's Books,
a division of HarperCollins Publishers, 10 East 53rd Street, New York, NY 10022.
www.harpercollinschildrens.com

The artwork was painted in acrylic on illustration board, then completed digitally.
The text type is 18-point Chalet.

Library of Congress Cataloging-in-Publication Data

Prelutsky, Jack.
[Poems. Selections]
The silver moon : lullabies and cradle songs / by Jack Prelutsky ; illustrated by Jui Ishida.
p. cm.
"Greenwillow Books."
ISBN 978-0-06-201467-2 (trade ed.)—ISBN 978-0-06-201468-9 (lib. bdg.)
[1. Children's poetry, American. 2. Lullabies, English—United States.]
I. Ishida, Jui, illustrator. II. Title.
PS3566.R36S55 2013 811'.54—dc23 2012038097

13 14 15 16 17 SCP 10 9 8 7 6 5 4 3 2 1
First Edition

 Greenwillow Books

For all the new dragon babies
—J. P.

For MOM (aka: Nihon no Obaachan)
and MIL (aka: Morris Obaachan)
—J. J.

The Train That Visits Dreamland

The train that visits Dreamland
Is chugging down the track.
It will not be till morning
That the train comes chugging back.

My baby rides aboard the train
Throughout the tranquil night,
Asleep with dreams of wonder
And infinite delight.

On the Forest Floor

On the forest floor, a cricket
Chirps the whole night long.
High above, an owl perches,
Whispering a song.

All throughout the silent trees,
A night wind softly sighs.
On the pond, a frog is croaking
Tadpole lullabies.

The Silver Moon

The silver moon shines softly,
The sun is not awake.
A beetle rows an acorn boat
Across a silver lake.

The acorn bobbles up and down
Beneath the silent skies.
The beetle soon grows sleepy
And shuts its tiny eyes.

Little Red Fox

Little red fox slumbers
safe in its den,

Little pink piglets
now sleep in their pen.

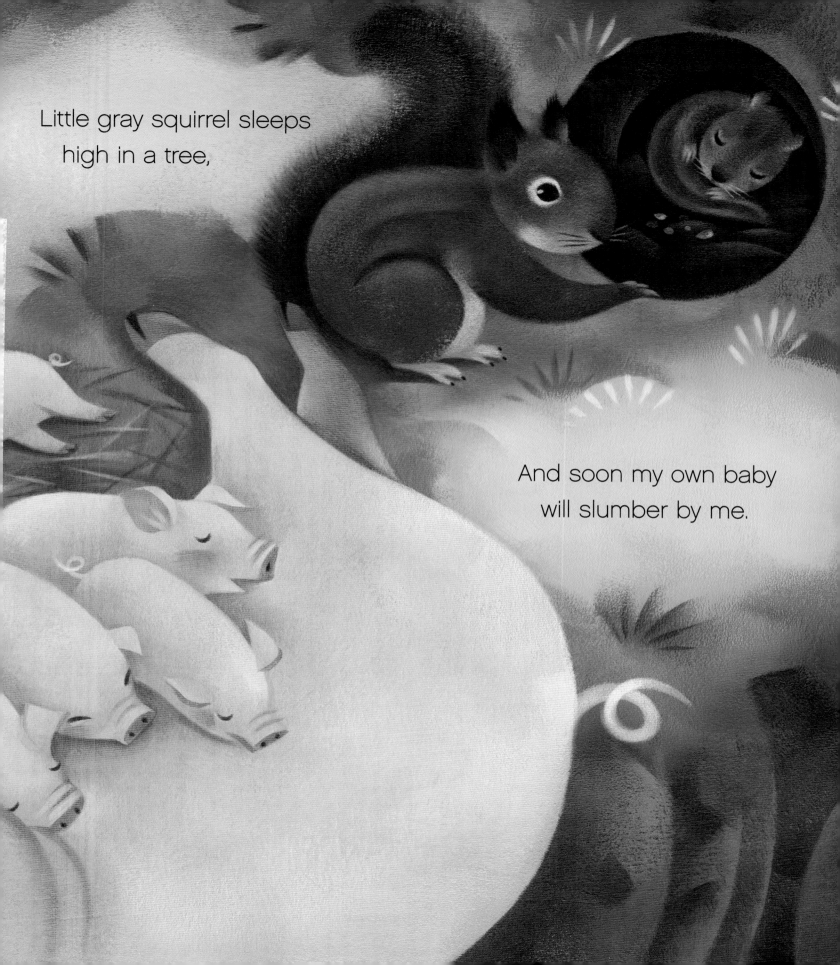

Little gray squirrel sleeps
high in a tree,

And soon my own baby
will slumber by me.

Rabbits Hop

Rabbits hop and hop and hop
Upon a velvet lawn.
They hop and hop throughout the night,
They will not stop till dawn.

And while the rabbits hop and hop
The starry night away,
My little baby softly sleeps
Until the break of day.

Bird Lullaby

Robin, jay, sparrow, chat, chickadee, wren,
Mockingbird, meadowlark, hummingbird, hen,
Oriole, bunting, crow, tanager, thrush,
Bobolink, swallow, are all in a hush.

Starling, swan, whippoorwill, pelican, pigeon,
Bluebird, finch, quail, warbler, woodpecker, wigeon.
None of them now make the tiniest peep,
For like my sweet baby, they're falling asleep.

Tadpoles Play Leapfrog

Tadpoles play leapfrog
And possums play possum.
Butterflies flutter
From blossom to blossom.

The world's full of wonders—
These are but a few—
And my little baby
Is wonderful too.

Underneath the Rising Moon

Underneath the rising moon
Gleaming in the sky,
Your loving mother sings to you
A tender lullaby.

Sleep in peace, my precious baby,
Never shed a tear.
You are the one in all the world
Your mother holds most dear.

The Waves of the Ocean

The waves of the ocean
Are washing the shore,
While I'm with the baby
I truly adore.

The beautiful stars
Twinkle high in the skies,
And my little baby
Is closing her eyes.

Go to Sleep, Baby

Go to sleep, baby,
My dear little dove,
Your father is rocking
Your cradle with love.

While feathery clouds
Are afloat in the sky,
Your father is singing
A soft lullaby.

My Dear Little Baby

My dear little baby,
The dearest on earth,
You've always been loved
Since the day of your birth.

Your mother adores you,
As any can tell,
And I am your father,
Who loves you as well.

Autumn Lullaby

The leaves are falling from the trees,
They're falling to the ground.
They fall so very softly
That they scarcely make a sound.

Go to sleep, my little one,
Never, never cry.
Your loving grandpa sings to you
An autumn lullaby.

Ten Little Fingers

Ten little fingers,
And ten little toes.
Two little eyes,
And a dear little nose.

Two little lips
With a beautiful smile—
One happy grandma
To rock her awhile.

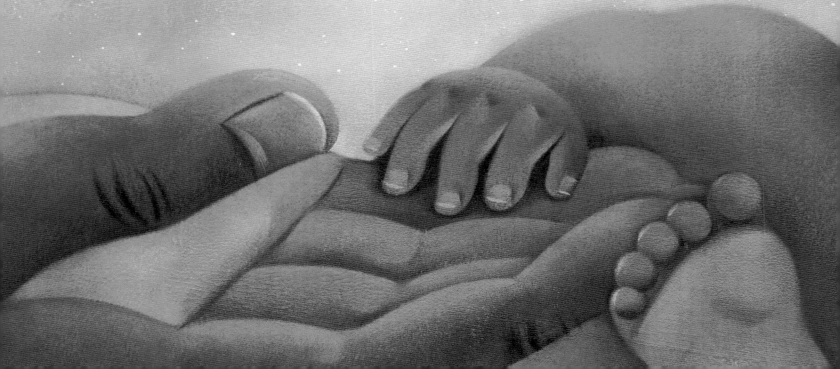

Outside the Window

Outside the window
In twinkling array,
Fireflies dance
A nocturnal ballet.
They flitter about
All throughout the long night,
Filling the air
With a beautiful sight.

They hover and soar,
Flying near and then far,
Each one a radiant
Miniature star.
And each little firefly's
Flicker and spark
Helps guide my sweet baby
To sleep in the dark.

In a Quiet Little Garden

In a quiet little garden,
Where the grass is green and deep,
A turtle safe inside its shell
Is almost fast asleep.

The turtle soon will slumber
Beneath the rising moon.
The dearest baby in the world
Will also slumber soon.

Lotuses, Crocuses

Lotuses, crocuses,
Poppies, and daisies
Have folded their petals
To sleep the night through.
The bees of the meadow
That visit the flowers
Are home in their hives
And are slumbering too.

Now is the time
For my beautiful baby
To be fast asleep
Like the flowers and bees.
So slumber, my dear,
Till the flowers awake
And the bees buzz about
On the crisp morning breeze.

Sheep Are Asleep in the Meadow

Sheep are asleep in the meadow,
Geese are asleep on the pond.
Deer are asleep on the hillside,
And in the valley beyond.

Bears are asleep in the forest,
Fish are asleep in the sea.
Birds are asleep on their branches above. . . .
My baby is sleeping by me.

Now the Night Has Fallen

Now the night has fallen,
Now the air is still,
Now the moon is shining
High above the hill.

Now the birds are silent,
There is not a peep.
Now my little baby
Soon will be asleep.

Hushaby, Baby

Hushaby, baby,
The night wind is sighing,
An owl is flying,
A whippoorwill sings.

Hushaby, baby,
I hope that my lullaby
Sends you to Dreamland
On gossamer wings.

Silently, Silently

Silently, silently,
All through the night,
My baby is sleeping,
Her eyes are shut tight.
She will not awaken
Till morning's first light—
Silently, silently,
All through the night.

The Silver Moon

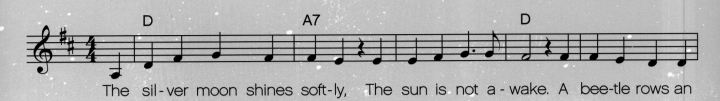

The sil - ver moon shines soft - ly, The sun is not a - wake. A bee - tle rows an

a - corn boat A - cross a sil - ver lake. The a - corn bob - bles up and down Be-

neath the si - lent skies. The bee - tle soon grows slee - py And shuts its ti - ny eyes.

Little Red Fox

Lit - tle red fox slum - bers safe in its den, Lit - tle pink

pig - lets now sleep in their pen. Lit - tle gray squir - rel sleeps

high in a tree, And soon my own ba - by will slum - ber by me.

In a Quiet Little Garden

In a qui-et lit-tle gar-den, Where the grass is green and deep, A___

tur-tle safe in-side its shell Is al-most fast a-sleep. The_ tur-tle soon will slum-ber Be-

neath the ri-sing moon. The dear-est ba-by in the world Will al-so slum-ber soon.

Hushaby, Baby

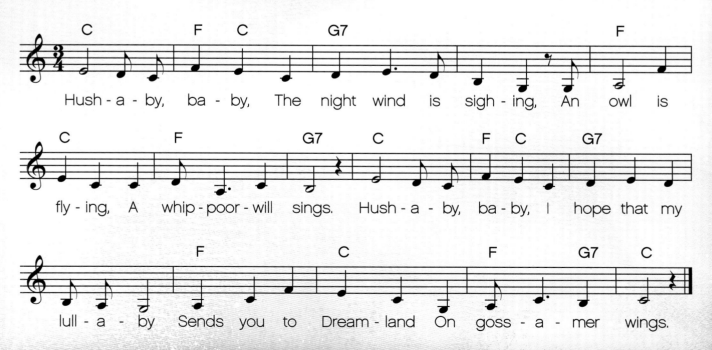

Hush-a-by, ba-by, The night wind is sigh-ing, An owl is

fly-ing, A whip-poor-will sings. Hush-a-by, ba-by, I hope that my

lull-a-by Sends you to Dream-land On goss-a-mer wings.

Visit www.jackprelutsky.com for additional music.